For the staff and pupils of Hyde Park Infant School, Plymouth, England
N. D.

For Anna, who opened my eyes to the beauty of things
S. R.

First U.S. edition 2012

Library of Congress Cataloging-in-Publication Data is available.
Library of Congress Catalog Card Number pending
ISBN 978-0-7636-5936-3

12 13 14 15 16 CCP 10 9 8 7 6 5 4 3 2

Printed in Shenzhen, Guangdong, China

This book was typeset in Cold Mountain Sx and Alghera.
The illustrations were done in mixed media.

Candlewick Press
99 Dover Street
Somerville, Massachusetts 02144

visit us at www.candlewick.com

Just Ducks!

Nicola Davies

illustrated by

Salvatore Rubbino

CANDLEWICK PRESS

Quack-quuuack, quack-quaack-quack.
It's the first sound I hear every morning.
The quacks start long and high and get
quicker and lower at the end.
Quack-quuuack, quack-quaack-quack.

I open my bedroom curtains.
Who could be making all that noise?

Ducks—just ducks,
down on the river
that flows through
the town.

Male ducks
quack so quietly that
you have to be close
to hear them.

Female ducks quack
loudly to call other
ducks to join them.

At first, there are only two or three of them,
but by the time I'm dressed,
lots more have arrived and are
preening and splashing
—and quacking!—
in the sunlight.

It doesn't take long for me to eat my breakfast,
but the ducks take forever to eat theirs!

When they preen,
ducks spread oil
from a little spot
just under their tails
all over their feathers
to keep them shiny and
waterproof.

They're STILL eating when I cross
the bridge to go to school.

I look down and
see them swimming
around, dabbling at the
surface . . .

"Dabbling" is when ducks nibble at the surface
of the water with their beaks to get tiny bits
of food—small insects and seeds.

and upending
to reach food that's
underwater. Brrrr,
it looks so
cold!

"Upending" is when ducks push their heads right under the surface to eat water plants and creatures such as snails.

11

We visit the ducks on the way home from school in the afternoon. When the weather's very cold, they're still hungry!

Usually, you shouldn't feed ducks, but they need more food when it's cold, so in some places people feed ducks bread in harsh weather.

Although ducks can't live on bread alone, it can help to keep their bellies full when times are tough.

I go down to the water, and
even though they're wild birds,
they come close, just to see
if I've got any food for them!

They're all mallard ducks, so the girl ones,
the "ducks," are streaky browns and tans.

The female's
quiet colors help her
hide from danger
when she's sitting
on her eggs.

The boys, called "drakes," have
glossy green heads, neat white collars,
and a cute little curl on
their tails.

They both have a secret
patch of blue on each wing,
which I see when they
stretch or fly.

Drakes don't sit
on eggs, so they
don't need to be
camouflaged.

I like it when a drake shows off his handsome feathers to the ducks, trying to get one to be his girlfriend.

Sometimes the drakes get very excited
and chase a duck in a gang or fight, splashing in
the water and making a big fuss.

From fall through winter, drakes try to find a mate in time for spring, when the ducks will be ready to lay their eggs.

In spring, there won't be as many ducks
on the way home, because they'll be busy nesting.
For almost a month, the mother ducks will
sit on their eggs, hidden away,
sometimes in some pretty
funny places.

Mallard ducks make
their nests on
the ground and
lay between
8 and 13 eggs.

Predators like to eat
eggs and ducklings,
so mother ducks
hide their nests
carefully.

Last year, one made her nest in our greenhouse!
When the ducklings hatched . . .

they had to climb the wall
at the back of the yard,
then jump down to follow
their mom to the river.

As soon as their ducklings hatch, mother
ducks get them to water, no matter what,
because they are safer there from cats
and other hungry creatures.,

19

But now it's getting dark.
The lights on the bridge begin
to glow, and all over town, people are
getting home for dinner. It's time for ducks
to find a safe place for the night.

Some sleep under the bridge.

Ducks usually sleep at
night because they can't see
to find food in the dark. But they
have to sleep somewhere
predators can't reach them.

20

Some fly off to roost in the reeds.
Some float on the water with
their heads tucked under their wings . . .

21

and SOME don't go to bed at all! I know,
because one night at choir practice, we heard them

If there is food to eat and
moonlight or street light to see by,
ducks will sometimes stay up late,
especially when worms come out
of their burrows at night.

quacking softly outside the window as they ate worms
off the lawn in the dark! Wak-wak-wak-wak-wak-wak-wak.

23

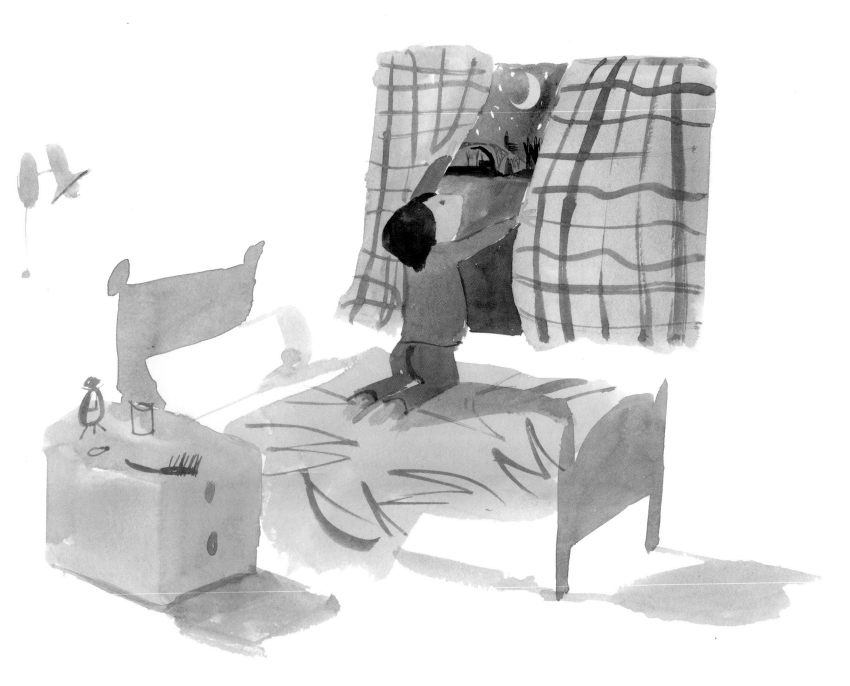

When I close my curtains on the frosty stars,
the ducks have disappeared. The bridge
is quiet, and there's just the sound
of rushing water and the stillness
of the night.

But in the morning, they'll be there . . .

QUACK QUACK QUACK QUAACK-QUACK

QUACK QUACK QUAACK-QUACK QUACK

ducks — just ducks,
down on the river
that flows through
the town.

QUACK

QUACK QUACK QUAACK-QUACK

QUACK

QUACK QUACK QUAACK-QUACK

QUACK QUACK QUAACK-QUACK

QUACK QUACK

QUACK QUAACK-QUACK QUACK

QUACK QUACK QUAACK-QU

Index

Look up the pages to find out about all these duck things.

Don't forget to look at both kinds of words —

this kind and this kind.

Dozens of Ducks

The ducks in this book are mallard ducks, which
are found all over Europe, America, and Asia, as
well as in Australia and New Zealand. But they
are only one of more than 120 different kinds
of ducks that live in every kind of watery place,
from river rapids to marshy ponds, and from lakes
to the open ocean. Although these many kinds of
duck have different colors and live in different
ways, they share a similar shape of body
and beak that we all know as—
just duck!